Alfie the Sea Dog

First published in 2008 by
Franklin Watts
338 Euston Road
London
NW1 3BH

Franklin Watts Australia
Level 17/207 Kent Street
Sydney
NSW 2000

A CIP catalogue record for this book is available
from the British Library.

ISBN 978 0 7496 7946 0 (hbk)
ISBN 978 0 7496 7958 3 (pbk)

Series Editor: Jackie Hamley
Editor: Melanie Palmer
Series Advisor: Dr Barrie Wade
Series Designer: Peter Scoulding

Printed in China

Franklin Watts is a division of
Hachette Children's Books,
an Hachette Livre UK company
www.hachettelivre.co.uk

To Lyn, James, and
especially Alfie – M.G.

Alfie the
Sea Dog

by Mick Gowar

Illustrated by Mike Phillips

W
FRANKLIN WATTS
LONDON•SYDNEY

Alfie was a sea dog.

He sailed the seven seas.

He cooked the
sailors' breakfasts.

He made them cups of tea.

And when the sailors
climbed the ropes,

or raised the big
white sail ...

Alfie sang a jolly song
and wagged his jolly tail.

The sailors covered up
their ears.

"Enough!" the captain roared.

"That really is an awful noise, I beg you, please, no more!"

Then one dark night,
far out at sea,
a new ship sailed along.

17

"More sailors!" Alfie
thought. "Goodie!"

"I bet *they'd* like my song."

So Alfie threw his head back,
to sing with all his might.

The pirates all threw
down their swords,

and raised their
hands in fright.

"Don't hurt us!" screamed
the pirate chief.

"We give up!" shrieked
his crew.

"We've caught you now!"
the captain cried.

So Alfie was a hero and
he sang his song all day.

The captain gave out
earplugs ...

... and the sailors cheered,

HOOray!

OOOOOOOO

Leapfrog Rhyme Time has been specially designed to fit the requirements of the Literacy Framework. It offers real books for beginner readers by top authors and illustrators.

Other Leapfrog titles also available:

Leapfrog Fairy Tales

A selection of favourite fairy tales, simply retold.

Leapfrog

Fun, original stories by top authors and illustrators.

For more details go to:

www.franklinwatts.co.uk